Cranberry Kisses

By Sierra Zinke

Copyright

Dedication

To the long distance besties who are the sunshine in the storm, the flowers in the desert, and the light on the darkest of days.

To Carla

Chapter 1: Harvest Season

It always amazes me that I live in a place that offers excused absences from school, to harvest cranberries. Now this is only offered to the farm kids and those who work on the farms in the summer but still, isn't our education important? Shouldn't we be learning about the mitochondria being the powerhouse of the cell, or civics? How to be a good citizen? Maybe some algebra or any type of math so we can balance our finances and have financial stability as adults?

No. It is the end of September. We are one month into school and for the next three weeks I will be giving marsh tours on our cranberry farm.

Don't get me wrong, I love our family farm and am so grateful to have this in our family. Grandma Sharon's great -great grandfather is the one who bought the property and started the farm originally, and it has stayed in our family ever since.

But I have dreams, I am moving out of this middle of nowhere, everyone is in everyone's business town. I dream of moving to Milwaukee, becoming a physical therapist, and making a difference in people's lives. After my ACL tear two years ago, this goal only grew because I now know the importance of being strict about the rehabilitation program and ensuring that the muscles and ligaments are strong and ready for the upcoming season. I want to apply that same strategy to help professional athletes not only recover from their injuries but be stable enough to prevent them in the first place.

Which is why I should be at school, and practice not trudging through eighteen inches of water showing people around the marsh and explaining the process.

Plus who the hell gives a shit about how cranberries are harvested?

"Olivia, let's go, the first tour is in twenty minutes!" I hear

my brother Carter yell from the bottom of the stairs. Carter is one

of the twins and the only one likely to take over the family

business. He is the most excited about harvest season and only

finished high school to take over the business.

I can't help but roll my eyes from inside my bedroom as I

pull out my dark green waders, and make sure to slide an extra pair

of socks over my leggings to try to stay as dry as possible. It might

still be mostly warm outside but the water is frigid. Pulling the

newest pair of green waders over my clothes I head down the stairs

to grab the Thermos of scorching hot coffee Mom usually leaves

on the counter before heading to the hospital. But there is no

Thermos.

"Who the fuck took my..." I start to yell, when Noah walks

in the front door with my Thermos pressed to his lips a slight smirk

on his face. Of course, he is here and of course, he is drinking my

coffee. Noah is Cole's best friend, also my social savior from

freshman year of high school.

They met on the soccer field as kids and have been basically inseparable since then. As a child I had a giant crush on Noah that slowly faded as we became closer in high school.

"C'mon, you know I'm a monster in the morning without my coffee. Do you really want to subject the poor tourists to that?" I say in an almost whiny voice reaching my arm out with grabby hands to indicate I want it back.

"I am on tour duty with you today for that very reason," Noah replies knowing very well that might be the absolute last thing that I want. I roll my eyes in response, already annoyed about the morning, and grab the back up Thermos Mom hides in the fridge for my mid-afternoon caffeinated pick-me-up.

"It's a full day of tours, Noah, you are responsible for any trauma they have afterwards," I say laughing lightly.

The cuckoo clock on the wall and yes, I mean a literal cuckoo clock, one of the ones where the damn rooster pops out on the hour and makes those god awful cock-a-doodle-doo noises. Yes, one of those, starts cooing which means we have about two minutes to get out to the barn before dad starts to lose his marbles.

After many years of complaining, yelling, and arguing, we as a family, really, just Penelope and I, convinced them to change it so it only coos once a day, when the farm day starts. We later had to compromise twice a day during harvest season to indicate the start and end of each harvest day.

"It's day one, we can't be late, your dad would literally end us," Noah says, securing the Thermos tightly in his grip. The corner of his mouth starts to curl up into a challenging smile and I instantly know where this is going.

I look down to make sure my shoes are on tight, grip the Thermos with all my strength and take off toward the barn. It has been tradition for years to race to the barn on the first day of harvest. It started when I was super young trying to keep up with Cole and Noah, when in reality they were probably trying to get away from me. We have raced every year since, and I never win.

Today that is going to change. It is my last harvest and my last race so I have to at least make it a close one. We race down the long dirt driveway smiling and laughing, I am shocked I'm actually keeping up with Noah. The distance from the driveway to the barn is probably the length of a football field, and I can see Dad, my brothers, and the three family friend workers' who help during harvest time standing at the edge of the barn watching us come barreling toward them.

Watching Cole and Carter bicker back and forth leaves no doubt in my mind that they placed bets on this race, and it looks like Cole might be the one winning today based on the hard, grumpy scowl Carter is giving me. I am actually going to win, just by a hare, but I am going to win. Until my foot slips in the mud.

I forgot we just flooded the field and that means everything is wetter, muddier, and more slippery than usual, and at the last second I slip in a patch of mud and start stumbling forward but falling backward all at the same time. Like my legs are moving too fast for my body and now I am going to be a muddy mess.

Right into Noah's arms. At the finish line. In front of my dad and twin brothers. One who also happens to be Noah's best friend.

And here we are, standing with Noah's arms entirely around me, huffing and puffing out of breath in front of everyone.

Chapter 2: Barn Brothers

Silence. There is literally nothing but silence. For what feels like an eternity. He caught me from falling in the mud and making a complete fool of myself before the tourists get here and the first harvest. Literally nothing else happened.

That is it.

Right?

I can feel Noah let go of me gently, but also quickly once he realizes I am on my feet and stable again. I murmur a quick "thanks" and then look at Dad for today's list of events. He is just looking at me with narrowed eyes and an annoyed yet skeptical stare. Carter looks ready to murder Noah, and Cole is laughing about how clumsy I am which is nothing new.

I look around to see Noah standing stiff as a board, arms now at his side pretending to act cool. He always says Carter terrifies him and that he really needs this job to help support his family since his father passed away just over three years ago. But now he looks like his entire world is upside down, entirely rocked, and going to end this very moment.

Cole punches him in the arm and says "what is wrong with you today?" noticing the awkward stiffness and position Noah is standing in.

"Your brother is terrifying. Look at him, he looks like he's going to drown me in the bog now for not letting Ollie fall," Noah replies, shaking out his arms as a shiver goes down his entire spine.

Cole laughs in response knowing that Carter is easily the most terrifying sibling we have. He is extremely protective over our entire family. When our older sister Penelope brought her now husband Jonathan home for the first time, you would think Carter was a detective interrogating him and all aspects of his life making sure he would be the right fit for Pen. But we also know Carter would never actually hurt anyone, or at least he hasn't yet.

"Good," Carter replies, remembering to continue the tough guy, scary scowl he always wears. It would kill him to smile more. Literally.

Dad just shakes his head with a silent chuckle and turns to walk to the big board in the barn office with this week's schedule. Every week during harvest he will take the smaller monthly calendar and put it on the giant weekly calendar on the barn wall so everyone can see it. It is broken up by time, job and person responsible for each task. Being the smallest and only female who participates in the harvest now, responsible for tours and then marketing out to the community and bigger vendors along with the photography portion of the tour. When I was in middle school I had a dream of becoming a photographer so my parents bought me a camera and built a photo aspect into the tours. Participants have the option to add in a photo package with their U-Pick time, where they receive a gallery of photos at the end of the day. This is the last month of tourism in Fisher Creek and the last chance for the farm to make money for the year.

We follow Dad quickly and all stand close by so he isn't yelling as he talks. He isn't old, but his voice is starting to get a little raspy. He has never been a yeller and will stand in disappointing silence before yelling. Which is arguably worse than just yelling at us in general.

Carter stands closest to Dad bouncing like a kid in a candy shop eagerly waiting for the sign to start the morning huddle. That is a task that was passed on to Carter as we start transitioning him to a leadership role; Dad isn't retiring anytime soon but now has an older daughter trying to start her family on the other side of the country in Georgia and it is important to him that he has someone trained to run the place if he decides to go visit.

Across from Carter stands Cole, still tormenting Noah who is standing next to him and then there is me standing next to Noah trying to look as annoyed as possible about the entire situation. For the last few weeks I have made it extremely clear I do not want to be involved in harvest season this year but standing here with the people who mean the most to me, I am feeling a little nostalgic that this will be the last harvest we get to all spend together.

Carter goes through the schedule for today, letting Noah and I know we have a total of four tours today, each approximately ninety minutes long with a thirty minute U-Pick included. Which also means I have double the work today getting the photos together for each group. I look at Noah, knowing this is his favorite type of tour because it involves genuine interactions and making connections with the tourists which is his cup of tea. He is definitely a people pleasing extrovert who is fully energized by these interactions, whereas by the end of today I will want nothing more than to curl up in my bedroom with a blanket, book and a cup of sleepy time tea. Great, now I can't stop thinking about how great the porch swing and my current read would be right now.

"Behave," I hear Carter end his speech by glaring at Noah and me. At least they have separated Noah, Cole, and I. We have been known to cause a touch of trouble along the way.

I roll my eyes at Carter and grab the keys to the golf carts tossing one to Noah so we can head out to meet our first group.

Chapter 3: Bog

Tour groups can range from two to eight people and the property is a total of a hundred acres so the carts are critical for traveling around the property.

The first tour of the day went without a hitch; honestly, I don't remember the last tour that was that smooth. We always meet the tour group out at the farm stand at the end of the property and then work our way through the entire process.

Harvest season is only three weeks out of the year so the most common question people ask is what do we do with the remainder of the year, and what surprises them the most is that it is a full-time job for seven months of the year. The planning process is methodical and can take a lot of time. The soil prep process is the longest part because we have to ensure it is the right acidity and combination of garden soil vs peat moss.

The harvesting process is what everyone is most excited about, especially since we are a wet harvest farm, which serves primarily local stores, restaurants, and town members. Once the cranberries are ripe and ready for harvest, we flood the field with water above the height of the bushes then Carter and Dad go through the next day with a machine to basically poke all the bushes so that cranberries fall off and float to the surface.

Once they are floating on the surface we are able to collect them and load them up to be sold. When we have tours, people are given the option to pick their own cranberries, in which case we give them a small snake to round them up and collect them in a small section of each field.

We have seven different cranberry fields we flood over the course of three weeks for harvest. They are designed to be ready at different times during the harvest season and we alternate the order each field goes, each year to preserve the soil and the plants.

As a child, wading through the various fields with the snakes collecting the cranberries was my favorite part of harvest but as I grew older the water temperature dropped about as quickly as my patience.

We get to the last part of the second tour where they are all handed waders and given the opportunity to harvest cranberries themselves. Kids are always chomping at the bit to get into the bog and families are full of smiles and laughter and it all caught on camera for them.

Noah thrives on this part of the tour the most because it is a personalized section where he can make connections with each individual person. It is amazing to watch the sunshine he brings to everyone's experience and you can actually see the change he makes in their lives.

I walk around the corner of the golf cart and cannot help but smile watching the two children frolic into the water. They freeze as soon as it becomes knee-height recognizing the rules we have in place to protect them. Noah is by the shoreline explaining to the parents how to scoop the cranberries into the circular net while also showing the kids different shapes they can make to capture the berries. I remember when he first started making animals with the net and the pure life changing joy it gave them. He is creating core memories for everyone involved.

This family asked for some action photos of them in the bog together. They are from San Diego and the fact that there are entire farms dedicated to cranberries is news to them.

I pull out my old Nikon, which probably needs to be updated nowadays and snap a few photos as they work together to collect as many cranberries as possible. The kids use their nets like Hungry, Hungry Hippos and the parents laugh and smile, leaning into each other full of love. Before I realize it, Noah has rounded the golf cart and places his arm on my shoulder like a proud dad. The action makes me want to one, roll my eyes at him yet again, and two, lean into his shoulder which almost gives me an ick because why the heck do I want to do that?

"Remember when you wanted to make a career out of photographing the harvest?" Noah asks, smiling.

I can't help but give a huff of a laugh and reply, "It was a far fetched dream that wouldn't be sustainable long term." My shoulders sag a little remembering how much I used to love the farm, and taking photos for families that made a difference to them. Now, it is just a required task of my bloodline that seems more tedious than useful. "Plus, no one would buy these things anyways," I add.

He gives me a disappointed and disgruntled look, clearly annoyed with what I said, and lowers his hand off my shoulder. Halfway through the movement I shift and his hand brushes the small of my back causing me to freeze instantly. He brings his hand to his side before adjusting the straps of his waders and heading back out into the water with the tourist. It's time to wrap up picking and show them to the processing center. Which is really just an old building where we store the cranberries until they are picked up at the end of the day.

I shake out my body to get rid of the tension from Noah's touch. He is completely unfazed by the entire interaction but I cannot seem to shake the feeling inside me, the desire for more.

The parents walk out of the water and ask, "How much would it be for all of the photos?"

Noah overhears from the edge of the bog and looks over his shoulder with a smug look that I want to smack off him but instead I just give a soft smile and shake my head. "They are included in your tour package. You'll receive an email with them all tonight," I reply, pulling the camera away from my body to give them a sneak peek.

The mom gasps, bringing her hand up to her mouth, completely surprised and amazed at how the photos turned out without any additional editing or changes to them. "You really should charge for these. They are absolutely incredible," she says in response.

Chapter 4: Avoidance

The remainder of the day I keep a minimum threefoot radius between Noah and I, trying not to be too obvious with my avoidance to offend him. I keep reliving the moment his hand brushed my back, the electric magnifying feeling deep inside my core.

I have always found Noah to be incredibly attractive. He is at least six feet tall, having hit a growth spurt in the last year, and while he is really lanky, his legs are essentially tree trunks from soccer in literally the best way. His eyes are this beautiful shade of light blue, and look almost gray when the light is right. And while somewhere deep inside of me there has probably always been a slight crush for him since the day he saved me from sure social death in high school, he is my best friend and I couldn't imagine life if he was anything else.

Until today.

Saving me, yet again, from the mud was the initial shock, a magnetic pull connecting us together, an unexplainable driving force creating the desire to push my lips onto his, and sink further into his touch. I really need to stop this thought process.

The sound of hushed voices coming from the back side of the barn snap me back into reality because my family is not quiet by any means, aside from my father. We operate on *"the loudest person is the one who is heard and acknowledged"* which is probably why Dad utilizes silence to get our attention.

However, this has also taught me that as the youngest, the easiest move is to be the quietest and sneak around listening to everything going on. Primarily for ammo against my siblings like bribing them to do my chores in exchange for not telling mom they were sneaking out or starting a new relationship. I didn't have to do chores for almost six months when Penelope started dating a new boy back in eighth grade.

Which is why when I hear hushed voices, there is not a second thought before I find myself sneaking up around the metal half wall separating the office from the remainder of the barn. Plastering myself up against the wall as close to the edge as I can to listen to the gossip.

Until I realize it's Noah and Cole, and they are definitely talking about me.

It takes everything in me not to jump out and chastise them for talking about me behind my back until I hear,

"Dude, she is basically your sister, what are you talking about?" Cole says louder than any other part of the conversation. There is the quiet noise of a gentle shove as Noah shoves Cole telling him to quiet down.

What are they talking about? Why is Cole saying that? I mean he isn't wrong, Noah treats me like a little sister most of the time, looking out for me, supporting me and always offering a listening ear. He was the first person to know about my first kiss, and how upset I was when I found out that Matt was just using me for that kiss. He responded worse than Cole and Carter both did, threatening to ruin his life as retribution.

"She's your sister. But I swear there's something there, it started today. I don't know, bro. She's been weird since our second tour today," he replies.

Shit, he noticed. Does he feel it too?

I have always been clumsy, especially when I am trying to multitask so pairing my ninja skills with the conversation I just overheard I am destined for failure. The nice metal bucket full of bristle brushes at the edge of the wall becomes the perfect tripping wedge.

As the bucket crashes over, I am thankful it's empty and that we haven't started cleaning the carts yet but also am totally and completely busted.

"Ollie?" I hear Noah ask with a hint of concern in his voice.

"Of course, it's Liv, who else would trip over an empty bucket" Cole replies laughing. "Liv how long have you been sneaking around there? " He laughs between words.

I can feel my face turn into a giant tomato as I stumble around the metal wall into the open area where Cole has since taken a seat to laugh at me further and Noah leans against the counter next to the carts, smirking at me.

Carter walks in the side door, with a clipboard and a large Manilla envelope on the front of it. The last order going out today must have just left. He pauses looking up from the clipboard on his way to office, and asks,

"What is going on here? Why does Liv look like a firetruck?"

"Oh, just embarrassing herself infront of her new found love," Cole laughs in response. I feel my face instantly getting even more red, and Noah punches him in the arm.

Carter just shakes his head and walks away. I swear, he is turning more and more into Dad every day. You know those ridiculous commercials where they say *"we can't keep you from turning into your parents*", the one where they teach people how to take selfies, etc. Yeah. That one.

That is Carter. Everyday.

You would never know that Carter and Cole are twins because they are the definition of polar opposites. Neither of them are super interested in leaving Fisher Creek but Carter has always been invested in the family business. He is the tallest, and slimmest of the four of us, but also the most introverted. He never had a lot of friends in school, but no one ever bothered him either. One because he's Cole's brother, and two because he has a mean streak.

Whereas, Cole, the Golden Retriever personified, was popular, average sized, on the varsity soccer team, and the most charismatic individual in the entire town. Cole is not book smart, but very common sense smart, and utilizes that to his advantage. He had no desire to go to a traditional four-year college, but knew he wanted to make a difference in people's lives.

Our mom is a nurse at the hospital thirty minutes away, closer to Milwaukee, our dad a farmer. Cole and I definitely got the primary traits of our mom, helping people, the desire to make a difference. Whereas, Carter and Penelope got the traits of our dad, tough, methodical and driven to make something.

That is how Cole ended up being the only paid individual on the volunteer fire squad here in Fisher Creek and Carter matured to take over the family business and make a difference in his own way.

As Carter closes the door to the office, Cole's pager goes off, indicating he is needed at the fire station, or there may be a fire call. I haven't yet figured out what the difference between the beeping sounds it makes.

So, he runs out of the barn, not even saying goodbye as he disappears.

Leaving Noah and I standing five feet apart in the barn staring at each other. In utter silence.

My stomach rumbles with hunger breaking the silence, and I realize I haven't eaten since right before the first tour started. I was too riled by the moment at the bog this morning with Noah, to even think about food at lunch.

"Want to get some dinner?" Noah asks with a kind, awkward smile, acknowledging the embarrassment I just embraced at the hands of my brothers, and the fact that I definitely overheard part of a conversation he wasn't expecting me to hear. He rocks back on his heels waiting for a response.

I pause, for probably too long before answering because there is nothing I want more than to head down to the burger joint by the lake and eat a big ole juicy burger with some sweet potato fries but also should I really be trusted to go to dinner alone with Noah after today? He is my brother's best friend, after all, and this desire for more of him is very new and I do not know how to handle or control it yet. Normally this wouldn't be a concern, as we often hangout with just us or us and Cole, and always after a long harvest day.

"Yeah, but only if we can go to Bobbers Burgers," I finally reply as I start to walk past him toward the house. Noah shakes his head, the hottest smirk across his face, not surprised at all by my demand for burgers after a long day in the marsh.

As I push past him, he smoothly turns on his heels and follows closely behind me to the house to hang up the work waders in the mud room.

I may be starving but over my dead body will I ever leave the property in my waders.

Chapter 5: Bobber's Burgers

The ride to Bobbers was the most uncomfortable ride I have ever shared with Noah. Typically, he will roll all the windows down, play the music too loud and laugh at me as I sing from the top of my lungs. But today, we drive in silence. I can only assume it is due to what I overheard him and Cole talking about.

There is a ding of a hanging bell as you walk into the only burger joint in Fisher Creek causing everyone inside to turn and see who's walking in. So, as we walk in we are greeted with smiles and waves from Mark, the owner and manager, and his wife, Melinda, who works the front end of the restaurant.

We have known them forever, their oldest dated Penelope in high school and their youngest is in school with me now. Seeing them instantly makes me smile, giving a warm friendly feeling of comfort and home. Melinda takes us to my favorite booth in the corner but also one that bumps against the window overlooking the lake. As she turns to face me then, back to Noah, she makes the same face she always does, silently asking me if we decided to finally start dating. Everyone in town asks us this and typically, I just roll my eyes and shake my head no, but today I hesitate to answer, which is my first mistake.

Her eyes get big as she walks away, and I instantly know she and Mark are going to be standing by the counter to eavesdrop on us the entire time. In my defense, today is the first time I have had a desire for more.

We order everything but the kitchen sink and while we are waiting for the food, I take a minute to take in Noah's features, his lightly tanned skin, the tall and lanky body that is toned in the perfect way. The slight crook in his nose from when it was broken during a soccer match. The light blue eyes with some ungodly long eyelashes that feel like they are staring into the depths of my soul, when in reality he is probably just wondering why I am staring at him. I smile up at him as I take in the light smirk coming across his face.

"Whatcha looking at, Ollie?" he asks in a sarcastic sort of tone, knowing full well I am looking directly at him. I notice I am feeling a little embarrassed about staring at him and being attracted to him all in one swift motion.

Smiling back in return, I throw a French fry in his direction and then ask with a little bit of hesitation "What were you and Cole talking about in the barn today?"

His smile fades and he looks down towards the table full of food and says, "I think you know."

"I have an idea but I want to hear it from you," I say.

"Ollie… you have always been my best friend's sister until today, watching you with that camera, the little scrunch on your face when you are focused, that I realized how god damn cute you are," he says and my face yet again begins to turn into the biggest heirloom tomato. I have to look away to stop my face from heating any further. I really need to find a way to control this because it couldn't be more embarrassing.

"Cute?" I ask,acting fake offended.

Noah scoffs and says "That is what you got out of everything I said?"

I just shrug in response, dipping a French fry into the famous homemade ranch Melinda makes. I am always amazed at how such a small town can have such phenomenal food, you'd think these amazing people would want to go to a bigger city, to make a name for themselves instead of staying in this one road, timeless town we call home.

"Cole told me you're planning on going to Marquette in Milwaukee next year, finally getting out of here huh?" Noah says, trying to change the subject as we finish up our meal.

"Yeah, that's the plan. Go to PT school, make a difference in people's lives. Get out of this town where there is no privacy," I say the last part is a little harsher than intended but that's the problem with living in a small town, everyone knows your business, and half the time it's before you even know it yourself.

We pay and begin walking towards the front door when Noah replies. "That means this is our last year at the harvest together." I can only nod in confirmation because the idea of leaving my best friend behind gives me a lump in my throat the size of Mount Rushmore and my eyes water as if someone is dying.

Noah senses the shift in my emotions and wraps an arm around my shoulder, pulling me close to his side in a way I have only ever thought as brotherly but he adds a twist this time pressing his lips to my hair sending an electric shock through my body, and quietly whispers "Let's go for a walk around the lake."

Chapter 6: Fisher Creek Lake

The lake is my absolute favorite part of Fisher Creek; it is incredibly peaceful, calm, and welcoming. This time of year, the water is a very dark blue green that can be murky and spooky at night or in the early morning when the fog is standing over the lake. The trees surrounding the lake are the perfect combination of evergreen, oak, hickory and dogwood to give a beautiful blanket of gold, red and purple over the forested area. I always look for critters swimming along the surface of the water. If you know where to look, you can almost always find a spunky family of otters, in the spring the pups always chase each other. I can spend hours sitting mesmerized by them.

The lake is our biggest tourist attraction for a calm peaceful weekend, full of fishing, swimming, barbequing, and family time. But, by the end of September when harvest starts, the water cools, marking the end of the busy season here in Fisher Creek. The remaining stragglers trying to get one final weekend in will often wind up on the farm for tours or at the playground by the lake looking for alternative activities.

As we find our way to the walking path that travels the park side of the lake Noah doesn't loosen his grip around my shoulder, making our walk a little staggered. He stands at least six inches taller than me so I have to take two steps to match his. The park is quiet today and if it wasn't cloudy the sun would be setting giving a light pink hue to the lake.

We walk in silence while I collect my feelings, knowing full well that Noah will make me talk about them once I collect myself.

He is big on the importance of expressing and talking about your feelings because you cannot control how you feel, but can control how you react to those feelings. This was something he learned in his time in therapy after his father passed and had some difficulty processing everything.

Once my breathing starts to steady, his arm falls from my shoulder to my arm as he stops us from walking motioning to the dark green wooden bench next to the path.

Before he can even say anything, I say, "It just finally hit me that I am leaving everything I have known and everyone who has supported and protected me throughout the years. What happens if I fail? Who is going to pick me up? Maybe you should just come to Milwaukee with me." I say the last part only half joking, because in reality starting a new life in a new city is terrifying.

"OMG, I'm sorry I completely word vomited that" I say quickly, hiding my face with my hands.

His face changes from caring and concerned to almost disappointed in a matter of seconds, and I instantly know it's a silly question.

After his father passed away Noah took over the role of taking care of his family, especially since it took over a year to pull his mom out of her grief ridden depression that shook the whole neighborhood. Noah's dad was a huge member of the community. His sudden death took everyone by surprise and devastated his family. He had just retired from being the mayor and was going back to being a community philanthropist when he had a sudden heart attack walking to his car from the town hall building.

Noah's mom went from being a lively, beautiful, high standing member of society to barely getting out of bed to feed herself let alone her children. Bec was barely eleven years old at the time and didn't understand what was going on. Noah was a junior and we had only been friends for a few months. Cole and I gave Noah any support we could and it only strengthened our friendship.

I remember the worst of it, Noah showed up at my house with Bec and said that his mom hadn't gotten out of bed in days. Bec wouldn't give her space because she was confused and scared, and his mom had yelled at Bec for the first time ever. She wouldn't stop crying. I went to the big standing freezer in the finished basement and found an ice cream cup. The ones that are half chocolate, half vanilla with the little wooden spoon. The spoon that you can still taste today. She scooped little bites into her mouth between broken sobs, but by the time the cup was gone, she had stopped crying, and Noah felt comfortable leaving to try to help his mom.

They returned hours later together, both of their faces puffy and swollen from the tears they shed. My family had just ordered pizza and welcomed them all in with open arms. I think that was the real turning point for them; there were a few other low, dark moments but all were easily pulled out of with a little love and ice cream. It was also the moment that Noah's family and my family truly became family and the endless teasing about us getting married one day. At the moment it felt entirely ridiculous and gross.

But it only took that once instance for Noah to immediately jump into the caregiver role and do everything to support and protect his family. So much so that he opted out of college and a career outside of Fisher Creek to make sure there were no more dark days, and always food on the table, which also meant he worked full time on the cranberry farm to help with the bills. He would have had a scholarship to play soccer at a traditional four-year college, but sacrificed it for the good of his family. Even though now, three years later, his mom is back on her feet, she hasn't missed a day of work, a sporting event, play, or doctor's appointment in over a year. She even decided to continue the legacy of their annual Christmas Eve party his father had put on every year.

Remembering that now as we sit side by side at the lake, one of our favorite places, the place our families have the annual BBQ Bash together and also remembering everything he has given up for his family, and that he likely wouldn't be willing to leave anyway. He is nothing, if not a loyal man. The most loyal one I know.

"Ollie…" he starts but his facial expression is full of sadness. "The city is only two hours away; you're not leaving me behind, and I will pick you up whenever you need me too." He looks at me as I tilt my head toward the ground.

"I know, it would just be nice to have a familiar face there," I say, trying not to sound too disappointed. I knew I should not have gotten my hopes up. There was no way someone like Noah Kneland would want to be with a high school senior who he took in as a friend to save from high school social suicide during freshmen orientation. His hand lifts from his lap, his index finger lifting my chin up so I am looking at him.

"I know what you're thinking because it is written all over your face, and don't think like that. Olivia, I want nothing more than to kiss you right now," he says with his hand still beneath my jaw. My body begins to heat from deep within my core, and I want to lean in, cup his face with my hands and kiss him but just as I move, he gently pulls away.

"You feel this too?" I ask hesitantly looking into his endless light blue eyes.

"Yeah, Ollie. I do," he replies. I don't know how to answer him but a solemn look crosses over his face as he continues. "But you're getting ready for college. Don't get me wrong, I want to kiss you and start this life but you have soccer, your senior year,

46

and then college ahead of you," he says calmly with a bit of sadness in his voice. "Plus, Carter scares the living hell out of me, so I need to talk to him first."

The last sentence makes me chuckle because while Carter is the dark scary black cat of the family, I cannot imagine him hurting a fly. Let alone someone who is super important to Cole and me. But he is right, we need to talk to Cole and Carter, and I need to get through this harvest and focus on getting into Marquette.

And I really don't want anything to come between Cole and Noah.

Chapter 7: Family First

Cole's car is parked in the driveway when Noah drops me off. It took some serious convincing but I was able to convince him I should talk to the boys first and then he can talk to them tomorrow before harvest. I see the barn light is on, so I head out to the barn finding Cole sitting on a barstool at the counter in the barn. I pull up the stool next to him and we sit in silence for a moment, me looking down at the counter.

Cole puts his phone down, looking at me with a concerned look before saying, "What's wrong, Liv? You look like you've seen a ghost."

"I like Noah. Like, really like him," I respond, almost whispering, trying to be brave in my answer. Cole has always been my biggest support system, but Noah is one of his best friends, so it is especially important to have his support. I need him to not only be supportive, but to help me tell Carter and the rest of the family, without wanting to beat up Noah. Because while it is important I have his support, Noah needs him too. Potentially more than I do.

"You what?" Cole says to me with his voice a combination between a normal term and a yell. Apparently being my biggest supporter doesn't apply to this.

"We just want to see where things go. But, Cole, I think I really like him. And your support is important to me. But he needs it too, he's your friend too," I say by adding a touch of neediness to my voice. Being the youngest has taught me how to change my voice for my benefit when talking to my brothers. No one wants a whiny little sister around.

"Liv, it's weird, he's like a brother," he says naggingly

"Ew, stop saying that. I'm serious, Cole, this is my last harvest season, I need to know if the hot junior who helped me from eternal embarrassment at freshman orientation could ever be more than just a friend," I reply.

"I will always support you, and Noah, but I will never get used to saying that about him. And if I agree to support this absolutely no kissing in front of me.," he says after a long pause and a huge sigh.

A huge smile crosses my face and. I wrap my arms around his neck, thanking him silently.

"Now, help me tell Carter," I say hoping he will come willingly.

"Ha! Not a chance, my payment for support and keeping my mouth shut will be to watch you two squirm telling Carter." Of course he wants me to "pay" him for being a decent human. I roll my eyes and huff at him in response, turning and walking away back towards our old farmhouse. It sits on a hill in the part of the property with a big pond behind it, that we stock every year with largemouth so we can fish during the summer for fun.

The white farmhouse is three stories if you count the basement, which we have finished into a "playroom" for us kids. I hate calling it that, it makes us sound like babies all over again. In reality, now it's used for hangouts, movie nights with friends, and family gatherings. There's white panel siding leading to a dark olive green roof that looks almost black, and the beautiful wrap-around porch in the front and side leading to a screened in porch on the side and back of the house. At sunset the colors of the sky often reflect off the brown of the porch illuminating the entire area. It is one of my favorite places in the summer to curl up with a blanket on a brisk night with a good book.

I can hear the crunch of the gravel driveway behind me as someone comes jogging up, presumably Cole, when he grabs my arm to stop me.

"I am really happy for you, Liv, you both deserve this happiness. I know Carter has the 'hurt my sister and die' speech down, so I'm going to leave that to him, because I know Noah won't hurt you, Liv. But don't break him into a million pieces either, okay?"

Chapter 8: Senior Year

As graduation approaches and I start to reminisce on this past year, I realize that senior year in Fisher Creek is a big ordeal. Believe me I would know, I've gone through this on two other occasions with Penelope and the boys. Which also means I do not have a lot of time to spend with Noah pursuing our relationship, which is both heartbreaking but also probably a good thing.

The remainder of harvest season was chaotic, running back and forth from work to soccer practice and then getting all of my school assignments done. The family continues to make jokes about Noah and I, but overall are happy as long as we follow the one rule my parents set into place, not during harvest hours.

When we told my parents, my dad initially just scowled at us acting like this big ole tough guy but then broke into a smile and said, "Come here, son" giving Noah a huge hug. My mom embraced me and said, "Livy, we are so happy for you."

Everyone acted like we made a big announcement about dating, but really we were just testing the waters. Getting our toes wet before jumping straight in and the fact that I'm moving at the end of the summer plays a huge role in our decision.

Noah is the epitome of a supportive boyfriend, never missing a soccer game, helping me write my college essay, asking my interview questions even when we both knew he was staying here in Fisher Creek. We have a rule that even with our crazy busy lives, we go on two dates a month.

Our first date night in November happens to fall on the same time as the Class S Championship game for soccer. I am incredibly nervous because it is the championship game and my last soccer game. I've already decided no matter where I go to college I am going to focus on my education and not play sports.

I do not have to be on the bus until 1:00 p.m so when Noah showed up at the house with a coffee and a muffin from my favorite local bakery, I was surprised but also relieved. He has always been a sense of comfort for me. I had woken up grumpy about not being able to stick to our original date plans.But he showed up on my front porch at eight am with my favorite breakfast. My heart melts in my chest full of gratitude and a desire to stand and kiss him. We decided to take our relationship slow to make sure this was exactly what we both wanted, but also until we figure out what the future holds for us.

"You still deserve a date even if we can't go to dinner," he drawls, handing me the coffee and the muffin and then pulling me close for a hug.

I have always felt the saying "it's the small things" to be a bit cliché until this moment, because in this moment I feel loved, and cared for in a way I didn't expect. We sit on the porch in the big swing, my legs draped over his under the beautiful green cable knit blanket my grandmother made for me for Christmas, talking about the book I am reading, and what books we both like to read. We vow to always share books together.

I think I love Noah Kneland.

We don't win the championship game which was absolutely devastating. My friend, Julianna and I laid on the field in tears for a few minutes after the match. Noah and Cole took us out to ice cream at the local creamery, let us bitch about the awful officiating during the game and even sat outside with us in the cold. Noah held my hand the entire time, squeezing it when I began to get emotional again, showing support.

Then the letter came.

Cole intercepted the letter first, seeing the mail man pull onto the property, and saw the large white envelope addressed to me from Marquette University. Story has it that Cole gave Noah a heads up before even giving it to me, because "there is no way they send a rejection letter that thick." I was furious at Cole for telling Noah what he didn't even know but in the end it was the best thing for him to do. It gave Noah the time to process the acceptance letter and also be supportive. Noah is nothing if not loyal, and while moving to Milwaukee is not ideal for him, he knows it is my career and dream and will do anything in his power to get me there.

"*I got in!*" I yell as I come running through the front door waving the packet in the air like a raging lunatic, on a frigid day in February. There had been at least a foot of snow fall in the last few days and I got out of school early, met Cole at the local coffee shop for coffee and muffins where he gave me my acceptance package and then headed home to tell the family.

As I rounded the corner, the lights were dimmed, and my entire family plus Noah's family were standing in the kitchen with a massive cake, cheering in response to my excitement. I couldn't fight back tears as I got closer and saw the congratulatory carrot cake, my favorite, made to perfection to celebrate. I later found out that it was Noah's idea to get everyone together for the cake and I couldn't be happier to share this moment with those who I love.

"I knew you'd get in. I am so proud of you, Ollie," he says into my burgundy red knit hat, that's damp from the snow, while engulfing me in the biggest hug.

It feels too soon to talk about what we will do when I move to Milwaukee. But the longer we wait the harder the conversation becomes and the more we put it off. Plus, he hasn't even kissed me yet. Does he even want to continue this? Whatever this is. It feels like a relationship. I know it is to me. I have no interest in anyone else, I want Noah, I want more. I feel electric, alive and complete when with him. I also feel very confused but still do not bring it up to him to avoid seeming like the desperate, clingy girlfriend.

❄ ❄ ❄

Graduation is approaching and we have one date left before it arrives. We are having a sunset picnic at the park part of the lake. After we eat, we're sitting on the quilt watching the sunset over the lake. The pink and orange sky reflecting perfectly over the lake. I'm sitting tucked snuggly into Noah's side, his arm planted around me to hold us both upright. With my head resting on the front of his shoulder, his resting on the top of my head.

My body is heating from the constant contact we are sharing, pushing to be closer to him, for his hands to trace my hips, cup the side of my neck. I tilt my head up to him, as he looks down to me, our faces mere inches away from each other. I lift up my hand to the nape of his neck, prepared to bring his lips down to mine.

This is it, we are finally going to have our first kiss. I can feel his body tense and heat against mine, confirming his need for more as well.

"Olivia?" I hear from behind us. In a brief moment of panic, I pull away from Noah, and turn to see a few girls from the soccer team coming down the hill from the top of the park. I create a bit of space between Noah and I as he huffs and looks forward at the lake with a scowl that could kill someone straight across his face.

"Oh, hi," I say in return, waving and trying not to sound annoyed at their appearance. I never really had friends at school, or within soccer and seeing them in public is a chore on a regular day, let alone right now, when they are interrupting what is potentially the best kiss of my life. They have zero sense of awareness, which only irritates me more, as they waltz down the hill toward our quilt and proceed to plop down next to me.

Everyone knows Noah and his family so they begin chatting with us about life and the upcoming graduation. We end up sitting with them for over an hour mingling before Noah says, "Ollie, we have to go, I told mom we'd pick up Bec from dance tonight."

I thought he was using this as an excuse for us to leave and get back to our date, but as we are packing up for the car, my classmates say, "Bye, Liv, see you at school tomorrow, hope to see you at graduation, Noah." And I realize that Noah has completely shut down, he is quiet the entire ride to the dance studio, only really talking with Bec as we head back to my house.

I go to give him a hug and lean up for a quick peck of a kiss as he drops me off at home, but he actively pulls away from the kiss, giving me a very light, half hug. I know something is wrong and when I go to ask he says, "Bec is here and I have to get her home."

He gets back in the car, I yell bye to Bec well, to the both of them really. Full of anger and confusion about what happened today and why he is acting so distant all of a sudden. Graduation is a week away and we have no plans to see each other before the ceremony. Standing in the driveway, watching his car drive away, I taste something salty hitting my lips, realizing that I have started crying. I have allowed Noah into my heart and am starting to second guess whether or not that was a smart move.

Chapter 9: Graduation

Fisher Creek High School is a small high school with only 320 students, give or take a few. The census seems to be dropping too as kids are leaving for college, not having families of their own right away and may not return to Fisher Creek. So graduation is a town wide event, right on the front yard of the high school. They put up a small mesh fence around a set of approximately four hundred chairs. Eighty of those for the graduation class and the remainder for their immediate family. Then anyone else is able to sit or stand outside that fence free of charge.

Being a family of six is hard because we only get four tickets maximum for graduation anyway, and we know grandma and grandpa wouldn't miss this for the world, plus Noah, his mom and sister. My parents are big on family so they give their tickets to another classmate of mine so their entire family can sit together and arrive at graduation over an hour early to set up our section of lawn chairs for everyone.

Front and center.

In the exact location I would prefer them not to be.

I love my family. I really do but they are the definition of a big, loud, obnoxious family. They are going to cheer and whistle and bring all of the attention to me, when in reality I just want this to be over and never have to come back to high school again.

Noah drops me off at the required time, pulls me in for a big squeeze hug, and whispers "I'm proud of you, Ollie" into my freshly curled hair courtesy of Penelope. I am grateful my big sister came home for this; after she moved away to college and met her husband Jonathon, who is also here, I feel like I never see her and talk to her anymore. It always makes me laugh that when she lived at home we were constantly at each other's throats. I am almost five years younger and always wanted her attention, whereas she just wanted me to leave her alone. After she moved out to go to college we continued to grow closer and closer. So, the fact that they flew in together from Georgia means a lot to me.

"Thanks," I whisper back, closing my eyes, the nerves increasing in my stomach like a tumbleweed whipping through the desert. I haven't told anyone that I am giving a speech tonight, I haven't even told Noah that I am actually the class valedictorian. I've always been competitive and it felt like the best way to ensure my enrollment in the Marquette Physical Therapy program to be the best in my class but I never considered the fact that I will have to speak in front of my entire town, family, and those I love.

I hear a knock on the window of the door where seniors are supposed to go in to line up and hide from all the attendants, and see Julianna, my friend from the soccer team, staring back and waving for me to come inside.

"I have to get inside, see you after?" I say as I start to pull away, our hands linking at the end.

"Wouldn't want to be anywhere else," Noah replies with a soft smile and a gentle squeeze of my hand.

Surprised that Julianna is still standing there, because while yes, we are friends, we are school friends, and soccer friends. I don't think we have spoken outside of those settings since we met on the field four years ago. She is from Fisher Creek but the far side of the town so we didn't know each other growing up. With being pulled from school every year three weeks in, it was hard to make those initial important connections in high school. And once the boys graduated I found myself feeling isolated for this final year, hanging out with Julianna and her friends during the school day but the friendship ended there.

I walk through the door and am suddenly embraced in the largest hug ever, arms stiffly pinned to my side as I was not expecting to be embraced and had no time to react to her movement.

"We did it, Olivia, we are done and get to leave this godforsaken town," she shouts with excitement. She is literally trembling with excitement.

"How many Redbull did you have before this Juli?" I ask with a slight smile and laugh as I peel her arms from my sides.

"Too many." She laughs. Julianna lives off those things, it is no wonder that she is visibly shaking from her caffeine high. She likes to down one right before a soccer game as some kind of pre-workout energy boost.

She turns, links my arm and starts dragging me down the hallways to the big auditorium where we meet to line up, where I sit at the table and start going over my speech in my head. The school approves the speech ahead of time so it's not like they would let me say anything to embarrass myself, the community or the school but the idea of standing in front of hundreds of people and speaking makes me want to vomit everywhere.

"Let's go, seniors, line up, it's time to go," one of the teachers shouts over the excited squeals, and chatter in the room. I feel like a zombie pushing through the day, unaware of what is happening around me. I stumble into my place in line, reminding myself to smile and for the love of all that is holy *do not fall*.

"Please welcome our Valedictorian, Olivia, to the stage."

I smile to myself and stand to walk to the podium at the stage looking directly at the large pod of people that call my own.

Their eyes are big, Cole's jaw in the grass, the moms' crying, and the very typical stone cold stare of Carter and my father. The one face I don't look at right away is Noah's because I am not sure I can handle another surprise without instantly bursting into tears.

I will forever be grateful I decided not to tell them anything because the looks on their faces are absolutely priceless, and I am beyond proud of myself at the moment. I stand at the front of the podium, taking in the crowd when my hands begin to shake.

"Hi, everyone, and welcome to the Fisher Creek High School graduation…" That statement is the last thing I remember about my speech until I hear the loud sound of applause and notice that there are very few dry eyes in the crowd.

However, there is only one person I see in the crowd, Noah, who gives me a curt nod, the biggest smile across his face doing those big ass slow claps you see people do in movies when they are excessively proud.

I can feel my eyes begin to water as I take a minute to acknowledge all that I accomplished this year.

Chapter 10: Cranberry Kisses

After graduation, we all head back to the farm as a big group. When we start driving down the gravel driveway, I can see the top of a big white tent in the side yard, and instantly smack Noah in the arm.

"What the hell is that?" I ask.

He looks at me, then looks into the back seat at Cole. The corner of their mouths turning up in unison.

"Absolutely not, I told you I didn't want a party. It's just high school," I drawl, knowing this is a losing battle, and the entire family is probably already at the house. I knew I should have suspected something was up when we made a pit stop for gas when the tank has more than a quarter left in it. Who the heck lives by the *don't ever let it be less than a quarter rule* anyway?

"Sorry, sunshine, you were outnumbered on this one," Noah responds by grabbing my hand and squeezing it for reassurance. Sunshine. He has never called me that before but every ounce of my body tingles and I don't want him to call me anything else ever again.

"I will never get used to that," Cole complains from the back seat making a fake gagging noise.

I make a point to lean a little deeper into Noah's shoulder just for the sake of annoying my brother. Because what else is the job of the youngest besides annoying her siblings, and making him squirm is one of my favorite things to do.

"Fine," I huff in response, mentally preparing myself for continued socialization with family and friends. There are large coniferous trees my great grandfather planted around the perimeter of the lawn hiding the lawn from the driveway. This is used to maintain our familial privacy during harvest season and when people are on the property. Honestly, it's brilliant but at this moment I absolutely despise them. Almost as much as I despise surprises, and not being prepared for what I am about to walk into. As we go to turn the corner around the trees into the lawn I'm sandwiched between the boys, each with an arm around my shoulders, as if they knew I was going to turn and run at the first chance I get.

We turn the corner and I realize this is not just the small family social circle graduation party I expected it to be. This is a party for what looks like the entire graduating class and their families. I am flooded with emotion, which is no surprise because I am the emotional basket case of the family. Mom always tells me that my emotions are like the ocean: big, strong, can be dangerous and damaging, but also incredibly beautiful. I try to think about that statement every time I am flooded with a wave of emotion but this time it is a combination of many emotions and I have no idea how to process them before having to interact with everyone.

I must be visibly panicked because Noah presses his mouth into the side of my head and whispers, "Breathe, Ollie."

I take a deep breath, close my eyes for a second, breathe again and then continue to walk under the tent where a group of kids from my class are taking photos with the *Congratulations Graduates* sign.

Not long after, I ease into the scene of the party and am truthfully grateful that my parents are hosting this for everyone. We eat too much food, start a wiffleball game, someone throws a water balloon at Carter, soaking him and starting what might have been the most epic water balloon fight ever.

As I am wringing the water out of my no longer curled hair, Noah comes up behind me wrapping a hand around the small of my waist, sending an electric pulse throughout my entire body. Smiling at me with his beautiful light blue eyes that shine like the sky with no clouds in it and says, "Come on, Ollie, I have something for you."

The sun is finally starting to set and the sky is this amazing variety of pinks, oranges and purples as he leads me to the barn, grabbing a set of keys, and heading to the cart. It isn't uncommon for one of us to ride a cart around the property: one for privacy, two to check on everything and three to kill time and have a little fun, so I don't even bat an eye as we move throughout the property.

Noah parks the cart at the edge of field three, the same field we started last harvest season at and pulls his arm around me to watch the sunset. At this point in the year, the plants are in full bloom. The small white, pink and red flowers engulf the entire field radiating into the colors of the sunset. I can't help but smile, loving this view, this person, and today.

We sit in the back of the cart, soft music playing from his phone watching the sunset for some time before he leads me to the edge of the field, places one hand on my waist, interlocking our fingers on our other hand and begins swaying back and forth, leading us into a slow dance.   When the song ends, he leads me back to the golf cart and pulls a small white paper gift bag out of the back of the cart. How did I miss that when we were driving out here?

Handing it to me, he says, "I got you something for graduation."

My face blushes and I respond, "Noah, you didn't have to do that."

"I don't have to do anything, but this is something I wanted to do," he responds by kissing my forehead quickly and quietly. "Now, open it!"

I pull out a small sage green leather notebook with a pack of the cutest pens. It is an absolutely beautiful notebook but there is a hint of confusion as to why he is buying me a notebook as a graduation present. Before I can even say thank you and express my gratitude, he says, "So we can write letters back and forth."

Pulling him closer to me, our foreheads meet together. I move one hand up to the top of his chest and then slowly to the nape of his neck.

I say, "Milwaukee is only two hours away, silly, we won't need to write letters."

He tenses for just a quick moment before our foreheads separate, and I push up onto my toes, kissing his lips. No longer willing to push this off or wait for his move.

His entire body tenses for a second before he relaxes and begins kissing me deeper. He releases my hand and places his other hand just beneath my ass pulling me closer and kissing me deeper.

The one hand tenses around my neck before he pulls away from my body, sharply. I pause looking up to him concerned, as if I did something wrong.

"Ollie..." He starts hanging his head.

"What? Did I do something wrong?" I ask, as I take a step back.

"What? No. No, Ollie. You didn't. But I need to tell you something," he replies, still looking down at the ground.

I just continue to look at him, remaining silent, not knowing how to respond.

"Ollie, I enlisted into the army," he says. I don't even recognize the sound that comes out of my mouth. Is it even a word?

"Bec is starting high school in the fall, she has a great group of friends and mom is finally stable. I can finally do something with my life," he continues, gripping both of my forearms, as water starts to well up into my eyes, and I taste the warm saltiness of a tear reaching my mouth.

"That's so exciting, Noah, we have all summer together," I say through the tears, thinking that Army Basic Training is like any other school starting around Labor Day.

"No, Ollie, I leave for basic tomorrow in Oklahoma," he replies with his voice cracking as he holds back tears to compliment what has become a waterfall of tears streaking my face.

I am truly proud of Noah for finally doing something for himself, doing something to advance his career and what greater sacrifice than helping to protect our country?

I am not crying because I am disappointed or sad. I am crying because we finally kissed after dancing around it for the last nine months, coming close only to be interrupted by family or friends.

We shared our first kiss and it sparked something utterly life changing in me. It leaves me wanting more, more of Noah in all aspects. More kisses. More of his hands tracing the shape of my ass, or pulling me close to his body.

We shared our first kiss and he is leaving.

Tomorrow.

I'm crying because we shared our first kiss, and I don't want it to be our last.

SNEAK PEAK at BEAUTIFUL

NOTES

Chapter 1: ***Prologue: 10 years ago, Milwaukee***

Olivia

Of course, it is raining in Milwaukee as our plane lands, it's not uncommon for it to rain in October here but after the last day I had, the last thing I want is more dreary sadness in my life.

Mason, Caroline, and Savannah are all sitting at the house waiting for my taxi to pull up. I haven't even told them the extent of what happened but I was getting on a flight and coming back to Milwaukee. Two days early.

Mason: I got chocolate ice cream.

Savannah: I got us some extra wine & gin for you.

Caroline: Amazon cart is full of rope, duct tape, and a human size garbage bag.

Our group chat continues to ping as I climb into my Uber for the long ride home back to the house. Milwaukee is generally 60 degrees in early October with a healthy mix of sun and rain. Today, it is raining, the temperature is only 50 degrees, and all I want is to curl up alone in my room and hide from society.

My phone starts vibrating with a phone call and I pull it back out of my pocket to see who is calling me. Noah's name rolls across my phone and a photo of the two of us from high school graduation fills the entire screen.

Oh, fuck no. I immediately rejected the call. There is not a chance in hell I'm answering that call. I would rather be thrown off a cliff before I talking to him again.

Noah: Ollie, answer the phone

If I wasn't in the Uber, I likely would throw my phone into the bedroom and pretend it's lost. My phone starts ringing. Noah, again.

Deny.

Noah: Ollie, please.

The Uber rounds the corner to my house and I can see my friends standing in the big picture window that overlooks our living room waiting. I don't know how I got so fortunate to have these amazing friends ready to go to war for me without even knowing the situation, but I also know I am not getting out easy after coming home two days early from the trip that was supposed to change my entire life.

I had completed the first half of my first semester as a freshman at Marquette, met three amazing friends, living together and talking about where our lives would take us.

Milwaukee is my new home, I try to tell myself, only half convinced I will be able to make a forever life for myself here. Anything is better than a cranberry farm, seeing Noah's family every day, being reminded that I was not enough for him, and explaining it to my family.

My life might be falling apart now but it won't be forever because Milwaukee is where I want to be. Not Noah's arms.

Or at least I am going to tell myself that.

♪♪♪

I don't remember when I went and retrieved the letter, the last letter that Noah wrote to me while in training. I don't remember what prompted Caroline and Mason antagonizing me to throw it away, rip it up, burn it, to just cleanse it from my life.

But I did grab the box of letters, I did grab the last one and I did rip it into shreds. Maybe it was the wine, maybe it was twelve missed calls and text messages from Noah before Caroline hid my phone, maybe it was the wave of emotions, the anger, the sadness, the confusion.

Chapter 2: Present Day

"C'mon Olivia!" I hear Caroline yell over the stereo system playing "Any Man of Mine" by Shania Twain. Ugh I groan to myself as I dig through my closet for my black faux leather pants and dark red top to wear to the bars tonight. This has been Caroline and Mason's mission for the last ten years, to help me get over Noah. Take Olivia out to the bars, wingwoman her into some nice man's arms and let the rest be history. If only it were that easy.

Don't get me wrong, I have been in other relationships over the years but nothing ever felt right. I typically let things fizzle out after a few months because there was no point in wasting anyone else's time or effort if it wasn't going to work in the long hall. I was perfectly happy with the random hookup here and then but in reality I could do it all myself anyways.

But Mason and Savannah have finally admitted they are into each other and have been together for almost four years now. I think Mason is actually planning to propose in the springtime. Caroline and Ben have been together for six months and things are definitely getting serious between them. I love my friends and I know they mean well but I really do not need to be in a relationship. I have my job, running and plans for my future. I am making a difference in people's lives and I want to expand that to as many people in Wisconsin as possible. I was just asked to present at a school regarding physical therapy and the different facets of it. Definitely no time for a boyfriend.

"Coming! Just curling my hair" I yell back as I frantically, trying to pull myself together as quickly as possible. I don't particularly want to go to the bar tonight but also don't want to disappoint Caroline. She has been the best rock of a friend I could have ever asked for.

♪♪♪

We were sitting at a small cocktail table in the back of the bar waiting for the transition from a casual bar to a dance party, when two guys walked in the front door.

"No, Caroline" I say sternly before she even gets a word out. Her big brown eyes shrink, and the glow of excitement fades into disappointment at my immediate rejection.

"Come on, Olivia" she exclaimed clearly annoyed. "When was the last time you got laid? You have needs. Needs that running can't fix. Plus look at this man."

This man was attractive, tall, athletic built, thighs that could shatter a watermelon. Don't even get me started on his biceps, holy heck. His blonde hair was short, and his brown eyes reminded me of the espresso martini we just ordered.

"I don't need anyone to fill my needs, that's what Vlad is for." I reply calmly. Vlad is my favorite teal vibrator who lives in the comfort of my night stand and is amazing at his job.

"Vlad is great but when was the last time you were with someone? And I mean someone who you actually connect with?" Caroline replies hastily.

Noah. Noah was the last time I felt truly connected to someone, and the fact that after nine years it still has this much of an effect on me makes me even more angry. I returned from Chicago and instantly threw myself into my school, my work and my friendships, promising to never get that close to someone again, especially when all they do is leave.

"I don't need to connect with someone, Caroline. I am happy with my solo lifestyle." I reply, she only frowns at me.

"You can't hate all men but Noah forever. It really is not healthy." She bursts out before walking out onto the dance floor with Mason, Savannah and her new boyfriend.

I hear something ding, but being in a crowded room I just assumed it was someone else's phone.

Ding. Ding. Ding.

My text sound continues to alert me of incoming texts, and although we have a no phone at the bar rule, everyone is dancing so I pull mine out to make sure everything is okay.

Noah: Hey

Cole: sooo I ran into Noah…

Cole: I'm sorry.

Noah: I heard you're coming home in two weeks, let's get drinks and catch up? I miss you Ollie.

"PHONE!" I hear Mason yell from the other end of the dance floor as I am being rushed by my entire group of friends. I have never been so happy to buy a round of shots if it means my phone gets taken and hidden until the night is over.

Why would he say that? We haven't seen each other in nine years and never say anything more than "Happy Birthday" or "Merry Christmas" in our texts.

I fake the biggest smile I can as I hand my phone to Caroline, to keep from breaking the rules when it dings a fifth time. Noah again. All she has to do is look at the screen to know we need more tequila.

About Sierra Zinke

I am just your everyday bookworm who happens to be a chiropractor, here in North Carolina. Anyone who knows me knows that if I do not have a book on me (either hard copy or an ebook) something is desperately wrong. I love reading Romance, Fantasy, Romantasy & Historical Fiction (yes I know that is the outlier, but no I cannot get enough, I just love them). But more than my love for books and reading, I love sharing my favorites with those around me. When I am not working as a healthcare practitioner, or nose deep in a book, I love love love spending time outdoors with my partner Daniel and our pups Maverick & Mabel.

Everyone who loves to read or write or all of the above has a book story. A book that changed their lives, a person who encouraged them to read or maybe even both.

Here is mine:

As a child, I spent every other Friday night and all day Saturday at my grandmother's house, Sharon. She was one of my absolute favorite people in the world and is who I contribute my love for reading and books to currently.

We would frequent Barnes and Noble to pick up STACKS of books, literally whatever books I was feeling that week. Then we would head back to her house, sit on opposite couches and read and read and read. Sometimes together, sometimes our own books but always books.

As I grew older, school took priority and I found I really had fallen out of the book world, my grandmother was suffering from severe dementia and having anything to bring me close to her was necessary. So I picked up Book Lovers by Emily Henry and will never stop reading again. It gave me a passion, a hobby, a love for something magical and a way to be close to my grandmother who we recently lost in November.

My book story is emotional. And I thank you if you read all of this but I promise I am not a complete sap!

www.ingramcontent.com/pod-product-compliance
Lightning Source LLC
Chambersburg PA
CBHW060508300726

48975CB00008B/2696